When You Go Walk

When you go walking,
what do you see?

I see red, orange, and yellow
leaves on the trees.

3

When you go walking,
what do you hear?

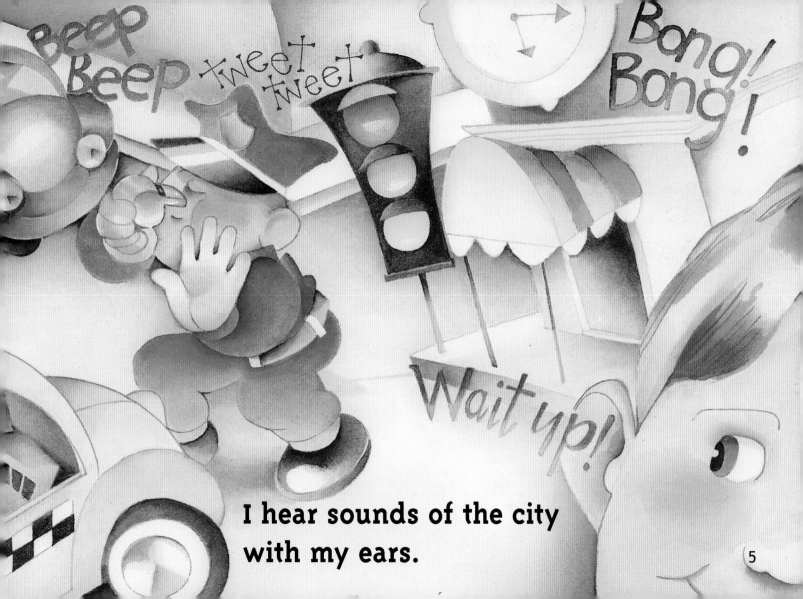

I hear sounds of the city
with my ears.

5

When you go walking,
what do you touch?

I feel cold water and soft sand.
I love it so much.

When you go walking,
do you smell the air?

I smell hot dogs cooking everywhere.

9

When you go walking,
do you taste anything?

I taste a little of everything!

When <u>you</u> go walking . . .

What will you see?

What will you hear?

What will you smell?

What will you taste?

APPLES

What will you feel?

And . . . what will you write about?

Your Turn to Write

1. When you walk around your neighborhood or go on a class field trip, take along a clipboard, paper, and a pencil.

2. Take notes about all the things you see, hear, touch, taste, and smell. Good writers take notes!

3. Use your notes to write and illustrate a five senses poem or a descriptive paragraph.

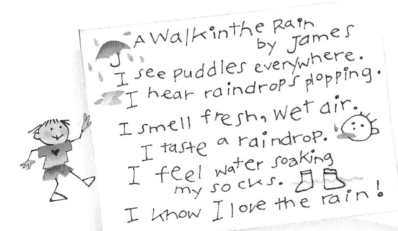

A Walk in the Rain
by James
I see puddles everywhere.
I hear raindrops plopping.
I smell fresh, wet air.
I taste a raindrop.
I feel water soaking my socks.
I know I love the rain!

My Trip to the Zoo
Our class took a field trip to the zoo. We saw my favorite animal... a cute cuddly Koala Bear. . . .